A Bed
Full of Cats

A Bed
Full of Cats

Holly Keller

Green Light Readers
Harcourt Brace & Company
San Diego   New York   London

First Green Light Readers edition 1999
Green Light Readers is a trademark of Harcourt Brace & Company.

Library of Congress Cataloging-in-Publication Data
Keller, Holly.
A bed full of cats/Holly Keller.
p. cm.—(Green Light Readers)
Summary: Lee fears he has lost his pet cat Flora,
until Flora returns with a new family.
ISBN 0-15-202331-3
ISBN 0-15-202262-7 pb
[1. Cats—Fiction. 2. Lost and found possessions—Fiction.]
I. Title. II. Series.
PZ7.K28132Bf 1999
[E]—dc21   98-55236

A C E F D B

Display type set in Fontesque
Text set in Minion
Color separations by Bright Arts Ltd., Hong Kong
Printed by South China Printing Company, Ltd., Hong Kong
This book was printed on 140-gsm matte art paper.
Production supervision by Stanley Redfern and Ginger Boyer
Designed by Barry Age

Flora is Lee's cat. She is as soft as silk. Flora sleeps on Lee's bed. Lee likes it that way.

When Lee moves his feet under the quilt, Flora jumps on them. *Thump!* When Lee wiggles his fingers under the sheet, Flora tries to catch them. *Swish!*

When Lee pets her, Flora purrs.
Purrrrrrrr…
When Lee sleeps, Flora sleeps, too.

One night Lee had a bad dream. He wanted Flora. She wasn't on his quilt.

He moved his feet, but Flora didn't jump
on them. He wiggled his fingers, but Flora
didn't try to catch them.
He wanted to hear her purr, but Flora
was not there.

The next day, Flora was not in Lee's room.
She was not on Lee's bed.
Lee didn't know where Flora was.

"You should try to look for her," said Mama.
"We'll help you," Papa said.
"She'll come home when she needs to eat,"
said Grandma.

Lee looked for Flora in the house.

Mama looked all around the garden.

Papa looked in the trash bins.

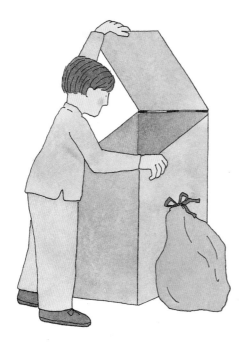

Grandma looked up in the peach trees.

Flora didn't come home. Lee was very sad.
His eyes were full of tears. If only Flora
would come back! "Please come home,"
Lee cried.

"We could put an ad in the newspaper,"
Papa said. "What should we write?"
"Write this," said Lee. " 'We lost our cat,
Flora. If you find her, please call.' Then give
our number."

Lee didn't hear anything about Flora. No one found Flora, and she didn't come home. Days and weeks went by.

Then one night, Lee felt something on his bed. He moved his feet under the quilt. *Thump! Thump, thump, thump, thump!*

He wiggled his fingers under the sheet.
Swish! Swish, swish, swish, swish!
Lee sat up and turned on his lamp.

"Flora is home!" Lee yelled. "And that's not all!"
Mama, Papa, and Grandma all ran to see.
There was Flora—with four kittens!

Now Lee has a bed full of cats, and he likes it that way. Those cats are as soft as silk. They are also fun. *Thump, thump. Swish, swish. Purrrrrr!*